The Problem with PROBLEMS

RACHEL ROONEY   ZEHRA HICKS

ANDERSEN PRESS

Problems are creatures.

They come in all sizes – from tiny to huge.

Some wearing disguises.

Knotty...

Hairy...

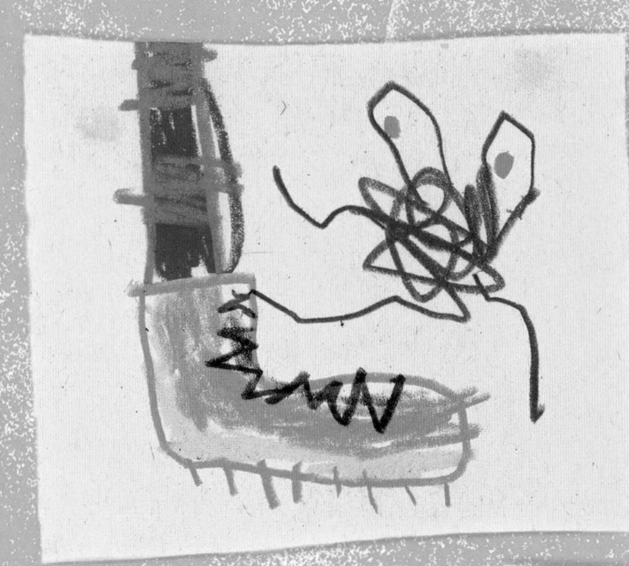

Slippery...

Tough...

Sticky like superglue, gathering stuff.

Each one is different – I've met quite a few.
But all of them want to make trouble for you.

They like to set traps.

They'll stand in
your way.

They turn the sky cloudy and paint the grass grey.

You'll find them in cafes...

playgrounds...

queues...

in boxes of toys...

and odd socks and shoes.

Whenever you meet one, don't worry. Relax.
Take a deep breath and consider the facts.

Have a good look at it.

Call it by name.

(A Problem is sometimes quite easy to tame.)

Look at it twice.

From a new point of view.

Maybe it isn't a Problem for you.

The small ones annoy you,
but often get bored.

They'll wander away when
they're being ignored.

Some need untangling...

CRASH!
WHAM!
BAM!
BANG!
BOOM!
PLINK.
PLONK.

Some slowly fade...

Others will wilt when they're
left in the shade.

Problems breed Problems.
Please keep them apart.

Don't feed them.
Don't pet them.
Don't take them to heart.

If ever you spot one heading your way...
try to avoid it. Don't ask it to play.

Some you can sleep on.
They wake in the night,

then quietly tiptoe and slip from your sight.

But sometimes a Problem refuses to go.

And, if that happens, it's handy to know...

Problems, like secrets,
are terribly shy...

They hate to be shared.
So give it a try.

On a bench...

On a bus...

On a bed...

In an ear.

You'll feel much better...

POP!
ZAP!

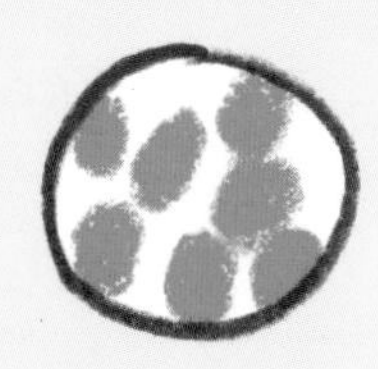

And they'll disappear.